Come Back, Amelia Bedelia

Story by Peggy Parish
Pictures by Wallace Tripp

P9-DYB-682

SCHOLASTIC INC.

New York   Toronto   London   Auckland   Sydney
Mexico City   New Delhi   Hong Kong   Buenos Aires

ISBN 0-439-54339-8

Text copyright © 1971 by Margaret Parish. Illustrations copyright © 1971, 1995 by Wallace Tripp. All rights reserved. Published by Scholastic Inc., 557 Broadway, New York, NY 10012, by arrangement with HarperCollins Publishers. SCHOLASTIC and associated logos are trademarks and/or registered trademarks of Scholastic Inc.

12 11 10 9   7 8/0

Printed in the U.S.A.   23

First Scholastic printing, September 2003

I Can Read Book® is a registered trademark of HarperCollins Publishers Inc.

For my favorite people
on 10 West

Judy Freedman
Jeanne Chernay
Rosemary Friedman

With much love-

"Oh, my cream puffs!"

said Amelia Bedelia.

She went to the stove.

"Just right," she said.

Amelia Bedelia took her cream puffs

out of the stove.

5

"There now," she said.

"I'll just let them cool.

Then I will fill them

with chocolate cream."

Mrs. Rogers came into the kitchen.

"Good morning, Amelia Bedelia,"

she said.

"Good morning," said Amelia Bedelia.

"I will have some cereal

with my coffee this morning,"

said Mrs. Rogers.

"All right," said Amelia Bedelia.

Mrs. Rogers went into the dining room.

Amelia Bedelia got the cereal.

She put some in a cup.

And she fixed Mrs. Rogers

some cereal with her coffee.

8

She took it into the dining room.

"Amelia Bedelia!" said Mrs. Rogers.

"What is that mess?"

"It's your cereal with coffee,"

said Amelia Bedelia.

"Oh, you are impossible!"

said Mrs. Rogers. "You're fired!"

"You mean you don't want me

anymore?" asked Amelia Bedelia.

"That is just what I mean,"

said Mrs. Rogers. "Now go!"

Amelia Bedelia

got her bag.

And she went away.

Amelia Bedelia walked toward town.

"Now what will I do?" she said.

She passed by the beauty shop.

A sign said **LADY WANTED**.

"Now let's see what that's about,"

said Amelia Bedelia.

She went into the beauty shop.

"Can I help you?" asked a lady.

"No, I came to help you,"

said Amelia Bedelia.

"Can you fix hair?" asked the lady.

14

"Oh yes," said Amelia Bedelia.

"I can do that."

"Then you can start now,"

said the lady. "Mrs. Hewes is waiting

to have her hair pinned up."

15

"All right," said Amelia Bedelia.

She looked all around.

"But I don't see any pins,"

she thought. "It's a good thing

I carry some with me."

Amelia Bedelia opened her purse.

She took out some pins.

And Amelia Bedelia began to pin up

Mrs. Hewes' hair.

"What are you doing!"

said Mrs. Hewes.

"Pinning up your hair,"

said Amelia Bedelia.

"Did I stick you?"

"Help!" called Mrs. Hewes.

18

The beauty shop lady came.

"Oh, no!" she said.

"What have you done?

Go away right this minute."

"All right," said Amelia Bedelia.

So Amelia Bedelia went on her way.

"Now why did she get so mad?"

said Amelia Bedelia.

"I just did what she told me to do."

Amelia Bedelia looked

in all the stores.

She came to a dress shop.

It had a **HELP WANTED** sign

in the window.

Amelia Bedelia went into the store.

"What kind of help is wanted?"

she asked.

"Sewing help," said the lady.

"Can you sew?"

"Yes," said Amelia Bedelia.

"I am very handy with a needle."

"Then come with me," said the lady.

She took Amelia Bedelia

into a back room.

"Please shorten these dresses.

They are already marked,"

said the lady.

"All right," said Amelia Bedelia.

The lady left her.

"I don't need to sew

to do this," said Amelia Bedelia.

She took the scissors.

And Amelia Bedelia shortened

those dresses.

Amelia Bedelia went back

to the front of the store.

"I'm finished," she said.

"What is next?"

"Finished!" said the lady.

"How could you be?"

The lady went into the back room.

She saw the dresses.

"Oh, no!" she said.

"You have ruined them."

"But I just shortened them,"

said Amelia Bedelia.

"Oh, go away," said the lady.

"I don't want you."

So Amelia Bedelia went.

"Some folks," she said,

"I just don't understand them."

Amelia Bedelia walked

another block or so.

She saw a sign in a window.

It said **FILE CLERK WANTED**.

"Now I wonder what a file clerk is,"

she said. "I'll just go in and find out."

A man met her.

"Are you a file clerk?" he asked.

"I will be one," said Amelia Bedelia,

"if you will tell me what to do."

"All right," said the man.

"First, take these letters.

They need stamps.

Then file these papers."

"I'll do that," said Amelia Bedelia.

The man went into his office.

Amelia Bedelia looked at the letters.

"Now should I stamp them all at once

or one at a time?" she thought.

"I better do them one at a time."

So Amelia Bedelia took each letter.

She put it on the floor.

And Amelia Bedelia stamped on it.

"There," she said.

"That should be enough stamps.

Now I better get these papers filed."

Amelia Bedelia looked at the papers.

Then she looked in her purse.

She found a fingernail file.

"It sure is small

to file all these papers.

But I will do the best I can."

And Amelia Bedelia began

to file the papers.

The man came back.

"Stop!" he said. "What are you doing!"

"Just filing your papers,"

said Amelia Bedelia.

"Do you have a bigger file?"

"Oh, no!" said the man.

"Do go away."

So Amelia Bedelia went.

"I declare!" she said.

"Everybody is mad today."

Amelia Bedelia

walked on down the street.

She came to a doctor's office.

There was a sign that said

HELP WANTED.

"Maybe that's the job for me,"

said Amelia Bedelia.

She went inside.

The doctor was there.

"I will be your help,"

said Amelia Bedelia.

"Good," said the doctor.

"Bring in the patients one at a time.

Come when I buzz for you."

"All right," said Amelia Bedelia.

"I can do that."

The doctor went into his office.

A woman and a girl came in.

"Who is the patient?"

asked Amelia Bedelia.

"Jane," said the woman.

47

"Then I'll take her in,"

said Amelia Bedelia.

She picked Jane up.

"Put me down! I can walk!"

screamed Jane.

"Nope," said Amelia Bedelia,

"the doctor said to bring you in."

48

And Amelia Bedelia carried Jane

into the doctor's office.

"Put Jane down!" said the doctor.

"Bring her mother in."

"Bring her mother in?"

said Amelia Bedelia.

"Can't she just walk?"

"Never mind," said the doctor.

"Mrs. Jackson, please come in."

Amelia Bedelia went back to her desk.

51

A little later the buzzer rang.

"I need your help," said the doctor.

"Dickie has a bad cut.

He needs a few stitches."

"I can take care of that,"

said Amelia Bedelia.

She opened her purse.

"Here is a needle. Now,

what color thread does Dickie like?"

"No! No!" said the doctor.

"I wanted you to put my gloves on.

Can you do that?"

"Oh my, yes!" said Amelia Bedelia.

"I will be glad to."

So Amelia Bedelia

put the doctor's gloves on.

"There now," she said.

"They're a little big,

but they're on. What next?"

The doctor looked at Amelia Bedelia.

His face turned red.

"Go home!" he said.

"Home!" said Amelia Bedelia.

"My goodness!" she said.

"I forgot about my cream puffs.

I must go back and fill them."

Amelia Bedelia went back

to the Rogers house.

"I'll just make the chocolate cream,"

said Amelia Bedelia.

She put a little of this

and a bit of that into a pot.

She mixed and she stirred.

And soon her chocolate cream

was cooked.

Mrs. Rogers came into the kitchen.

"That smells good," she said.

"Well," said Amelia Bedelia,

"I'll just fill the cream puffs.

Then I will be on my way."

"Oh, no!" said Mrs. Rogers.

"I'm sorry I got mad.

Please come back, Amelia Bedelia.

We miss you."

60

"All right," said Amelia Bedelia.

"I will be glad to."

Mr. Rogers came into the kitchen.

"I'm hungry," he said.

"Amelia Bedelia,

please heat me a can of soup."

"All right," said Amelia Bedelia.

She took a can of soup.

She put it in a pot.

And Amelia Bedelia

heated that can of soup.